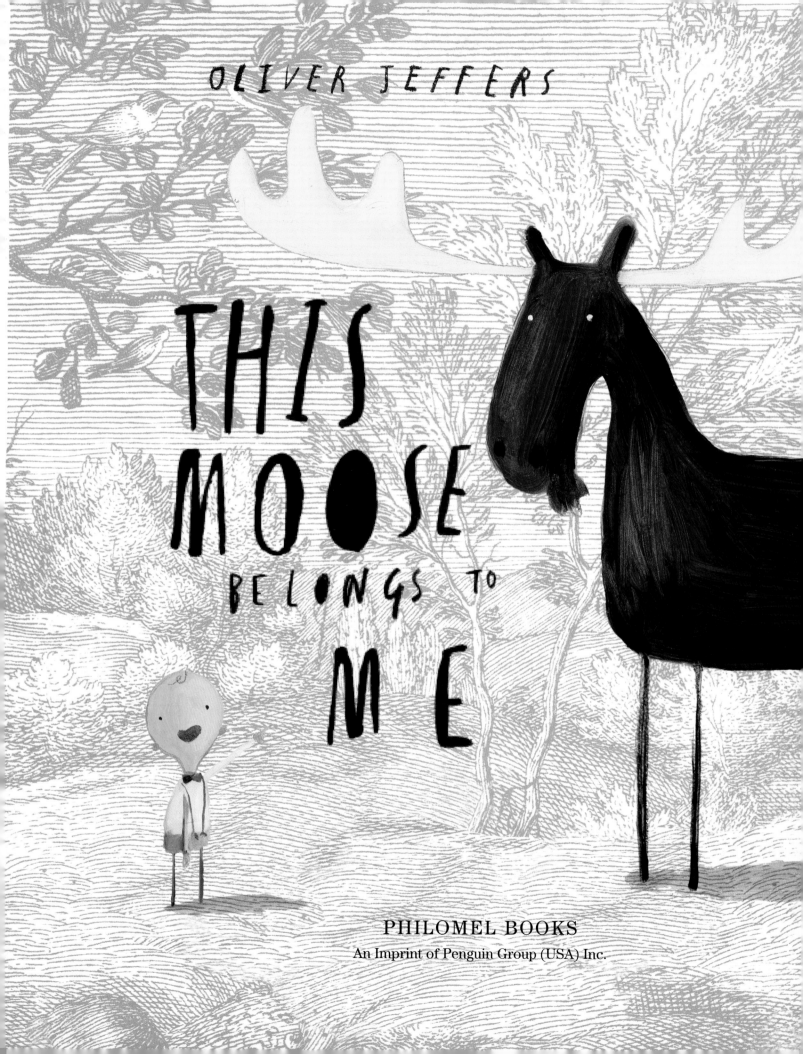

OLIVER JEFFERS

THIS
MOOSE
BELONGS TO
ME

PHILOMEL BOOKS

An Imprint of Penguin Group (USA) Inc.

For
MAC and ADRianna

PHILOMEL BOOKS

A division of Penguin Young Readers Group.   Published by The Penguin Group.

Penguin Group (USA) Inc., 375 Hudson Street, New York, NY 10014, U.S.A.

Penguin Group (Canada), 90 Eglinton Avenue East, Suite 700, Toronto, Ontario M4P 2Y3,
Canada (a division of Pearson Penguin Canada Inc.).

Penguin Books Ltd, 80 Strand, London WC2R 0RL, England.

Penguin Ireland, 25 St. Stephen's Green, Dublin 2, Ireland (a division of Penguin Books Ltd).

Penguin Group (Australia), 250 Camberwell Road, Camberwell, Victoria 3124,
Australia (a division of Pearson Australia Group Pty Ltd).

Penguin Books India Pvt Ltd, 11 Community Centre, Panchsheel Park, New Delhi - 110 017, India.

Penguin Group (NZ), 67 Apollo Drive, Rosedale, Auckland 0632, New Zealand
(a division of Pearson New Zealand Ltd).

Penguin Books (South Africa) (Pty) Ltd, 24 Sturdee Avenue, Rosebank, Johannesburg 2196, South Africa.

Penguin Books Ltd, Registered Offices: 80 Strand, London WC2R 0RL, England.

The art for this book was made from a mishmash of oil painting onto old linotype and painted landscapes,
and a bit of technical wizardry thrown in the mix here and there.

Library of Congress Cataloging-in-Publication Data is available upon request.

ISBN 978-0-399-16103-2

10 9 8 7 6 5 4 3 2 1

Wilfred owned a moose.

He hadn't always owned a moose.
The moose came to him a while
ago and he knew, just KNEW
that it was meant to be his.

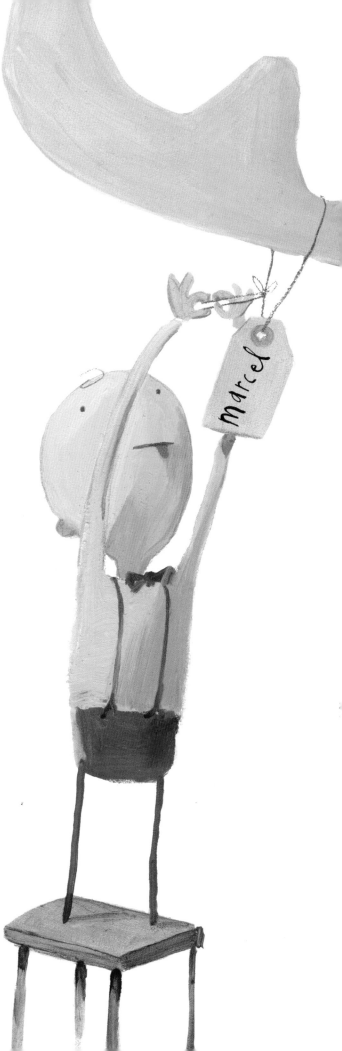

He thought he
would call him
Marcel.

He began following Marcel,
explaining the rules of how
to be a good pet.

Much of the time, it seemed as though the moose wasn't listening, but Wilfred knew he was. Mostly because he followed *Rule 4* very well:

NOT making too much NOISE while Wilfred plays his RECORD collection.

Sometimes the moose wasn't a very good pet.
He generally ignored Rule 7: going
whichever way Wilfred wants to go.

The moose had a very good sense of direction, and Wilfred did not. And because the moose was particularly poor on Rule 7 [subsection b]: MAINTAiNing a certain proximity to home, Wilfred quickly learned to bring some string along on their outings so he could find his way back again.

Sometimes the moose was an excellent pet. He had no trouble with RULE 11: providing shelter from the RAIN.

Marcel

Or RULE 16: Knocking down things that are out of WILFRED'S reach.

One day, as Wilfred discussed their plans for
the coming year on a particularly long walk,
he made a terrible discovery . . .

Someone else thought
she owned the moose.

RODRIGO!
you're BACK!

Wilfred was dumbstruck.
This moose was Marcel, not Rodrigo.
The old lady was mistaken and
Wilfred thought it only proper
that he correct her.

This MOOSE Belongs to ME!

he explained.

And to prove it, he called Marcel.

But the moose did not respond.
He seemed more interested in
the old lady.

good Rodrigo.

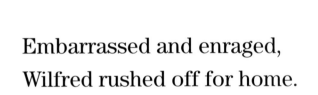

Embarrassed and enraged,
Wilfred rushed off for home.

But in his haste, and
miles from anywhere, he
tripped over his string
and got tangled up.

And there he lay.

Wilfred was beginning to get a little bit worried.
It was getting late and the monsters
would be out soon.

He had just
ruled out the
last of his options . . .

. . . when along came the moose . . .

. . . and performed RULE 73 brilliantly:

Rescuing your owner from PERILOUS SITUATIONS.

All was forgiven.
And perhaps, Wilfred admitted,
he'd never really owned the
moose anyway.

With that in mind, he and the moose reached
a compromise. The moose would agree to all
of Wilfred's rules . . .

. . . whenever it suited him.